The House

Across the Street

Jules Feiffer

Michael di Capua Books • Hyperion Books for Children

For Alice and Hal

Across the street from us there's a big, big house

where it's better than here.

There's a boy who's a little older and bigger than me.

He gets up in the morning as late as he wants.

And he doesn't have to go to school if it's raining.

He can eat on the expensive rug in front of the TV.

He can eat with his elbows on the table.

Or doesn't have to eat at all. If he gets hungry later, his mother brings him a snack in bed.

He bosses his big sister and his baby-sitter around.

And his mother too, but only if it's important.

He wins every game, he never comes in second.

He's all of his friends' best friend.

He's got a bike that's way better than mine.

And he's got four dogs: a schnauzer, a Lhasa,
a black Lab, and a Great Dane as big as a lion.

He's got a lion.

Okay, I'm exaggerating.

But he does own a huge tank of fish.

One of them's a piranha.

He can climb any tree in his backyard that he feels like,
and no one warns him not to.

He swings from the highest branch like Tarzan,
and drops feet first into the pool—

which causes a splash that empties half the pool,
including the dolphins.

And floods the backyard, including the dogs.
They don't mind, they laugh.

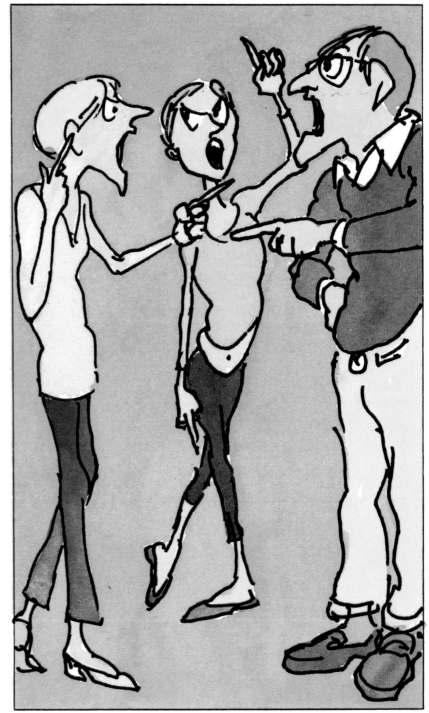

Everybody laughs in his house.   Nobody argues. Or if they do

they stop when he says so.

His parents love him so much!

But they don't show it by hugging and kissing
and fussing with his clothes.

They show it by calling every 800 number
on TV that advertises stuff he needs.

And they order it.

In the summer the whole family and the dogs and the piranha and the shark and the dolphins go to Maine on vacation.

The house is empty.

We don't go away, except for a week, or when we're invited,
but when we're not, which is most of the time . . .

I go across the street.

I walk back and forth in front of the house.
I'm not hurting anything.

Sometimes I knock on the door.
I know he's not there.

I just pretend he is.

I pretend he invites me in.

We become friends.

Some nights I sleep over.